TALENT
SHOWDOWN

nickelodeon

THAT GIRL
Lay Lay

TALENT SHOWDOWN

BY JEVON BOLDEN

ILLUSTRATED BY DEANDRA HODGE

SCHOLASTIC INC.

LAY LAY name and likeness © 2022 Fresh Rebel Muzik LLLP. All Rights Reserved. © 2022 Viacom International Inc.

All rights reserved. Published by Scholastic Inc., Publishers since 1920. SCHOLASTIC and associated logos are trademarks and/or registered trademarks of Scholastic Inc.

ISBN 978-1-338-77961-5

10 9 8 7 6 5 4 3 2 1   22 23 24 25 26

Printed in the U.S.A.   40

First printing 2022

BOOK DESIGN BY SALENA MAHINA

TABLE OF CONTENTS

·◆· CHAPTER 1 ·◆·

THE BEGINNING OF A NEW week at Woodlawn Middle School was like any other middle school week—unless you're a viral social media sensation like me. It was Tuesday, and I had just gotten into the building after an exciting Labor Day weekend in the studio recording a new collab with a high-profile producer and rapper. We even recorded some behind-the-scenes video that I got to show on my social media channels.

As I walked down the hallway to my locker, I

noticed that almost every kid I passed was staring and smiling at me like I was a blue unicorn or something. Kids must have seen the videos I posted this weekend. One kid even tried to sneak and snap a picture, but I was ready—I struck a cute pose and kept walking. I'm always ready for a cameo.

I mean, like, for real. What is my life? Sometimes I can't believe how much things have changed since my dad posted that video of me freestyle rapping in our car. One day, I was just Alaya High, a regular girl, going to school and hanging out with my friends. Now everybody with a smartphone and YouTube knows me as That Girl Lay Lay. I'm literally famous!

After the freestyling video blew up, I was invited to perform everywhere, and I now record albums in the same studios as some of my favorite artists. Still, I'm just the same girl who loves to go to school and hang out with her friends. Being semi-famous won't change that.

It seems like everything happened overnight, but it was a lot of hard work, practice, and believing in myself. With school and everything, it's not easy juggling it all. It's a task, but what else would I do? This is the life I was made for, and I love it. I truly believe everyone has the potential to be anything they want to be.

I mean, what?! Your everyday girl here, Lay Lay, just living her best life and manifesting her dreams—and doing it all with my girls at my side. There's Giana, who's been my BFF forever; amazing gymnast Akila; sweet-as-cotton-candy Riley; and, last but certainly not least, organic beauty guru Harper.

I love my girls. We are fun, smart, talented, and so supercute in our own unique ways. We have one another's backs, too. So much has happened for me in such a short time that if I didn't have my friends—well, I'd still be bomb, don't get it twisted—but it wouldn't be as much fun or nearly as manageable. They hold me down. I couldn't wait to see them at school that day!

And like clockwork, as soon as I rounded the corner to my locker, there they were.

Harper was the first to spot me. "Oh my gosh, Lay Lay!" Her long, silky black hair was pulled into a tight ponytail at the top of her head. Her dewy skin looked perfectly flushed in all the right places, like she'd just stepped out of a steam room.

Akila whipped around, her long, dark braids flying as she grabbed my hands and started jumping up and down. Soon Giana and Riley were in the mix, too. We all squealed and melded into a jumping, screaming, hugging girl cloud.

"Did y'all see the videos?" I asked when we settled down. "What'd y'all think?"

"Oh, Lay Lay! It was everything." Riley looked at me starry-eyed. She hugged her notebook close to her shirt, which read NAMASTE. Then she swept a lock of her curly ginger-red hair from her eye and tucked it behind her ear.

"You are so big-time, girl," Giana added. "You were spitting fire like crazy. I don't think the big boys could keep up." Giana was all about the details—she was a little nerdy but still had her own cool vibe. Her wavy, dark brown hair, hip glasses, crop top, and big baggy jeans let you know she was never to be taken lightly. Giana has been my bestie since elementary school.

"You were so focused and just . . . I don't know—on?" Akila felt around for her words. "It was like you were a whole other person." She loves to see people in their zone, you know? Athletes, performers, and especially fashion designers and magazine editors—she has a whole thing about reading their memoirs and watching documentaries about their lives, which I think is what makes her one of the smartest, most creative people I know. She works so hard to be great at everything. From gymnastics to schoolwork to her flawless braids, in her own quiet way, Akila Ojo was goals.

"It was so amazing, y'all!" I said. "I was a little nervous, but the producer and the other artists made me feel really comfortable. Everybody was so nice and professional." I was getting giddy all over again thinking about it.

"So what's coming up next?" Giana asked.

"Hey, did you guys hear?" Harper interrupted. "They're shutting down Hayes Theater."

"What?" Riley said. "No way!"

"Yeah, so you know my mom is on the board,"

Harper continued. "I overheard her talking about a real estate developer with a plan to build up historic Woodlawn and make it 'more modern.' He wants to tear down Hayes Theater and make room for a new living-shopping-eating lifestyle community. The theater just doesn't fit his vibe, so it will be torn down."

"How did I not know about this?" I was shocked for real. "My cousin Tasha works part-time in the theater's outreach department—and I'm there with her practically every day after school."

"I guess they've been talking about changes to historic Woodlawn behind the scenes for a while now. The city pressured the theater board members into a meeting with the developer this past Saturday morning. So Tasha may not have heard yet."

Akila's face fell. "This is really terrible," she said. "They can't just do that, can they? I liked going down to help with costumes whenever they had a show."

I knew how much Akila loved the Hayes. Of her many goals, being a fashion designer or costume designer someday was number one.

"Yeah, and I liked helping out with concessions," Riley said.

"We all liked that, too," I agreed. My mouth watered just thinking about my girl Riley Smiley's vegan treats. They are the bomb.

"I think they can and will," Harper said sadly. "They don't know or care about the history behind the theater."

We had all volunteered at the historic Hayes Theater before. My cousin Tasha and Harper's mom were always recruiting us. It was our chance to be involved in our community while doing the things we each loved. Harper probably helped out there the most. She used her beauty skills to do hair and makeup for almost every show. Akila loved to shadow the costume director, and she was the costume props assistant on the last musical at the Hayes. My bestie Giana had helped with sound and lights for the last few performances, too. And of course Riley donated her amazing organic desserts, baked with love at her family's farm. Whenever I could be there, I assisted the stage manager and helped Tasha with outreach.

Hayes Theater had been part of Woodlawn life for almost one hundred years. To hear that they were closing it down was the worst news to start the week. Though I was feeling kind of tired after my big weekend, my heart started pumping with the injustice of it all.

"We can't let this happen. We have to do something."

"I agree," Harper said, her dark eyes flashing. I could tell she was feeling fired up. "If the five of us put our heads together, we'll come up with an idea."

"Maybe Tasha can help, Lay Lay," Riley said. From the tone of her voice, I knew she was getting heated, too. "We need to find out if there's any way to convince the real estate developer that Hayes Theater is a valuable part of our community, and that it can't be torn down."

"I can talk to her today," I agreed. "Harper, what about your mom? Does she know anything more?" I was hoping we could get a few things working at one time.

"Oh, you guys know how she is. She's always stressing, but I'll see what she says."

Just then, the bell rang.

"Okay, we'll talk more in third period," I said.

We went our separate ways—well, everyone except Harper and me. We were both on our way to Ms. Ortega's language arts class.

As we walked, my mind was racing. There had to be something we could do. Hayes Theater was one of those places where people with different talents and backgrounds could all come together and do really amazing things. What would Woodlawn be without it?

·✦·· CHAPTER 2 ··✦·

MS. ORTEGA HIT THE LITTLE gong that sat on her desk. She usually lets us chat for a few more minutes after the bell rings. Then, instead of clapping, tapping, or shouting over us like a lot of teachers do, she uses the gong's sound to call us back to focus, as she would say. Today, its meditational ring pulled me back to the present from my thoughts about saving the theater.

I love Ms. Ortega. Language arts is my favorite subject, and she makes it even more awesome.

"Okay, class! Everybody okay?" she asked with a smile. Then she made eye contact with as many of us as she could—a little scary, yes, but that's Ms. Ortega. She likes to make sure we all feel "seen." Oh, do we ever.

"I want to give you a heads-up that this month we're going to shift from what we've been reading into some of my favorite works by Latinx authors," she continued. "September 15 to October 15 is Hispanic Heritage Month. You all know I like my kids to learn about the cultures of the world, especially those that reflect the backgrounds of the people who live right here in Woodlawn."

Sofia Montalvo raised her hand, as expected.

"Yes, Sofia?" Ms. Ortega asked.

"Can we bring in our own books?"

"Of course! Maybe we'll have a special day or two for show-and-tell, when you can talk about books you're reading by Latinx authors. But you have to read my stuff, too. Deal?"

Sofia beamed as she eagerly wrote notes in her binder.

Harper and I gave each other the side-eye, knowing this was totally Sofia's thing.

"So go ahead and get into your groups," Ms. Ortega said. "Let's continue working through the discussion questions for last week's reading."

As we moved into our groups, Terrell bumped my elbow with his and said in a half whisper, "Hey, I saw your video this weekend. You're really out there doing it big, aren't you?"

"Yeah, and . . ." I said. Terrell could get on my nerves. He's cool sometimes—we've known each other since elementary school. But I wasn't exactly sure where he was going with his comment, so I didn't want to let down my guard.

"It must have been nice to be in the room with those headliners. You really held your own."

"Thanks, Terrell." I managed a smile to hide my surprise. If I wasn't such a good actor, my jaw would have been dragging on the ground. I must be doing really well for the boy who teased me every day in elementary school to give me a compliment.

I got to my group and settled into our

discussion, but it wasn't long before the bell rang, and I was off to Mr. LaCourt's math class. Honestly, though, my thoughts had swung back to the Hayes Theater. All through math, I had trouble focusing on fractions because my mind was spinning, thinking about how to save the theater. The rest of class passed by like a puffy cloud. Math phased into musical theater, where, hopefully, my friends and I could talk about what we could do to help.

"Hey! Hello! Welcome back, everybody! Come on in." Ms. Duncan waved her arms as she directed us into her classroom like an air traffic controller.

Kids filed in like zombies, offering sleepy marshmallow-mouth greetings to our teacher. It wasn't even lunchtime yet, but I guess I wasn't the only one who'd had a busy weekend.

"Go ahead. Take your seats quickly. I have an

exciting opportunity I want you all to be part of."

As we slid into our seats, Ms. Duncan weaved in and out of the rows of tables, laying a colorful sheet of paper on each of our workstations.

Kids started to chatter as they discovered what was on the flyer. I hurried to my seat and grabbed mine to see what the fuss was about:

"Ooh," I squealed to Riley, Akila, Harper, and Giana, who were sitting at the same table as me. "This is so bomb! We should totally do this."

"Uh, Lay Lay, first, who is we?" Harper asked.

"And second," Giana added, "yeah, not me."

"What do you mean?" I asked, surprised. "Giana, you, Akila, and I did the talent show in elementary school. Maybe you're just a little nervous."

I couldn't believe my girls were shook, especially Harper. She is normally up for anything.

"Not really nervous, Lay Lay, but you weren't—

WILDCATS TALENT SHOWDOWN

WOODLAWN MIDDLE SCHOOL'S *HYPEST* NIGHT OF THE YEAR

PLAY * SING * DANCE * RAP * ACT * RECITE * PAINT/DRAW

ALL TALENTS WELCOME

WINNERS GET TO PERFORM THEIR WINNING ACT LIVE ON NEWS CHANNEL 19

SHOW US WHAT YOU'VE GOT!

REGISTER IN THE MUSICAL THEATER ROOM

DEADLINE TO ENTER: FRIDAY AT 3:00 P.M.

TICKETS: $5 IN ADVANCE; $7 AT THE DOOR

you know—you then," Giana said hesitantly.

"Huh? What do you mean? I've always been your girl Lay Lay." I wasn't understanding.

"Well, now, you're, like, that girl Lay Lay," Akila said. She looked down, drawing her finger in swirls on the table.

"Oh, you guys, c'mon! I'm still just Lay Lay."

"Lay Lay, it may seem like that to you, but what will everyone else think about our un-star-studded selves trying to get onstage with you?"

Giana looked me in the eye as she pushed her glasses firmly onto her nose. She knew how to cut right to the chase.

"They're going to think all of you are amazing and talented, too. That's that on that." I humphed, crossed my arms and legs, leaned back in my chair, and looked at each of them. I dared them to say something else even a teeny bit down on themselves again.

"Well," Riley tried to inch back into the debate. "We've only been lip-synching to stuff and doing bad copies of TikTok dances for fun. How will we be ready for a talent show in less than three weeks?"

"Y'all, c'mon." I was willing to beg. "Y'all know we are the bomb. With a little practice, we could easily take the prize."

Was I being too optimistic? I mean, I remember how awkward it can be to perform in front of the school, but this could be really fun. The girls would get a taste of my life, and maybe I could live my new life with my friends instead of always feeling like I'm missing out on something.

My thoughts were cut short by Ms. Duncan calling for our attention up front.

"Okay, everybody, this looks like fun, right? Dr. Lieberman, the band teacher, and I thought this was a great way to showcase the amazing talent at Woodlawn Middle. One of my good friends from college is a producer at News Channel 19 and has agreed to reserve a spot on the five o'clock news one week after the talent show for our winners. In addition to being on TV, we see this as a chance for our school to give back to our community with the money that's raised."

On cue, my friends and I looked at one another,

exchanging wide-eyed expressions. Could this be what we could do to save Hayes Theater?

"Yep," Ms. Duncan continued, "as part of your registration for the talent show, you must name a local charity or cause you believe in and write a one-page essay explaining why the school should support it. The essay is due with your entries this Friday. A week before the talent show, the entire school will vote for the charity that will receive the proceeds. If you'd like some ideas of what our city needs, Dr. Lieberman and I have some suggestions. Mainly, we want you kids to let us know some of the things you care about."

Oscar Tomlinson raised his hand. "Umm, Ms. Duncan? What if you don't have a talent?"

"Why don't you bring in those stupid cat-rats you're always talking about?" Brendon Evans yelled out from the back of the class.

"They're ferrets!" Oscar snapped back.

"Hey, now, Brendon. We're not going to do that." Ms. Duncan got him all the way together.

"Ms. Duncan, I'm a writer—I write plays and scripts," Sofia said as she pushed up her glasses and sat up straight in her chair like she was about to give a speech. "But that's not a talent I can show."

"These are great ideas. You're all really thinking," Ms. Duncan encouraged. "The goal is to be creative and think about collaborating with other students. Sofia, maybe there's someone who likes to act who would like to have an original monologue to showcase at the talent show."

"Ohhh!" Sofia beamed.

The class got a little chatty as ideas started to flow.

"Listen, everyone," Ms. Duncan said, raising her voice to get our attention. "This is not something you have to do by yourself. This is a great time to come together and let your talents complement someone else's. So choose your collaborators wisely."

"Yeah," Riley spoke up, "like Lay Lay raps, and, um, while baking is my thing, I can sing a little bit, too."

I couldn't believe it. Did she just . . . ?

"And I can produce music," Giana offered.

Next it was Akila saying, "I can design our

costumes!"

What was happening? Were my girls rising to the occasion? This was amazing. The way things were shaping up, everyone would soon see what I see in my friends. Though we each have different talents, this would be the perfect way to show them off *together* and save an important part of history at the same time.

I sat back in my seat, marinating in the moment. All I could think was *Tuh, these kids are not ready for what the five of us are about to bring.*

·✦· CHAPTER 3 ·✦·

THE LUNCHROOM WAS AS CHAOTIC as usual. Akila, Giana, and I each made it through the lunch line while Riley and Harper headed to our usual table near the center of the room. I grabbed my tray and started walking over, observing my classmates on the way. There was Brendon Evans shouting his video game stats to his gamer crew, and Emily Friedrich and her friends practicing TikTok dances between bites.

I saw Mr. Brown, the assistant principal, make a

beeline toward Oscar Tomlinson, who had just slid into line on his Heelys. Totally not dress code. *Got 'em!* I thought.

I could tell the word was spreading about the talent show because Reggie Johnson and his squad were beatboxing and freestyling. I overheard them talking about plans for their act.

"And then we can all come out and get in a circle and start flowin'," Terrell said.

"Yeah, straight off the dome like those old-school cyphers," said Dominick.

"Bruh! This is about to be so dope," Terrell agreed.

Reggie called to me as I passed him, "Hey, Lay Lay! What do you think? We got a chance at winning the talent show?"

"Y'all sound good, but my girls and me about to come with it, too. Y'all might not be ready for that!"

"Oh, really! You might be right, Lay Lay, if it's just you. But your girls? I don't know," he said with a sly smile. "The fellas and me are coming correct, ya heard!" He cupped his hands around his mouth like a megaphone for that last part.

They all started hyping one another up and yelling out "Yep, yep!" and "Let's go!"

"Umm, hold up." I put my hand out like a crossing guard halting traffic in a school zone. "I need y'all to recognize that we will not be coming to play. Okay? So if you are coming at all, y'all better come correct."

I like talking a little noise with the boys. My friends and I had a long way to go to get our slumber-party, singing-in-the-shower act ready for prime time, but I certainly wasn't going to let Reggie or anyone talk bad about my girls.

"Hey, Lay Lay! C'mon, girl! We don't have all day." Giana called me over to the table, interrupting my thoughts. The rest of the girls were all there and were in deep by the time I sat down. The only topic of conversation was the talent show and how we could help save Hayes Theater.

"Okay." Harper let out a big sigh as she opened up her lunch. "This is kind of scary and super exciting at the same time—eeee!"

"Wait a minute—are those what I think they

are?" I eyed Harper's lunch, too distracted to move on. Her mom makes the absolute best fresh Vietnamese spring rolls.

Harper grinned as she pushed the container toward me. "I packed extra just for you, Lay Lay."

"Thank you, thank you, thank you!" I grabbed a spring roll and turned back to the task at hand. "First, we need to write this essay about why Hayes Theater should be saved. Then we choose a winning song to make sure we can get on News Channel 19 to let everyone know what's happening."

"I could start writing the essay about Hayes Theater now," Harper said between bites. "Then we can each add our thoughts to it."

"Oh yeah, that's perfect, Harper," Riley said as she dug into a delicious-looking salad she had brought from home. "Maybe we can do flyers, too, to pass around the school next week before we all vote."

"I like that idea," I said, getting psyched up. "I can work on the flyer. Y'all know I'm kind of nice with graphic design and photo editing. Plus, Tasha has access to color printers at the theater. What about the song?"

"Well, we've been playing around with a few of those '90s hip-hop songs just for fun. Could any of those songs work for the talent show?" Giana said.

"Whatever we do, it has to be a winner," Akila inserted.

"What about the song Riley leads?" I asked as I picked up my slice of school lunch pizza. It really didn't compare to Mrs. Pham's spring roll.

"Oh no." Riley turned as red as a tomato. "I was only kidding around."

"No, don't back down now, Riley! You sounded so confident in Ms. Duncan's class." Giana lightly elbowed Riley and winked.

"Yeah, Riley!" Akila chimed in. "You really do have a nice voice."

"What about the dancing part?" Harper asked.

"Maybe we can come up with something together," Akila said. "I know a few moves from my gymnastics routines that might work."

"Okay!" I said. "This is sounding good."

"Yeah, it has to be good. Hayes Theater is not going to save itself," Giana said fiercely.

"And a good performance is really important," Akila said. "So whether we think we can do this or not, we have to at least act like we got it going on. Confidence is going to be key."

I could feel my friends both slightly freaking out and really getting excited. "I think we'll surprise ourselves with what we can accomplish together."

"It'll be great," Giana said. "We just need to do what Ms. Duncan said. If we each contribute something special, this will be one incredible act."

"Yeah, we can totally do this!" Harper said.

"So what's our group name going to be?" Akila asked as she played with one of her braids thoughtfully.

"Oh yeah," we said all at once, deflated.

"Listen, we can worry about that later," Riley said, perking up. "We don't need a name to choose a song, and we don't need a name to start practicing."

She had a good point.

"Yeah, the name can come later," I agreed. "When can we all get together to practice? Let's see . . . Akila has gymnastics almost every weeknight except Wednesday. I've got like two shows a week for the next month . . ."

"Don't we all have Saturdays free?" Giana offered.

"That will work," I said. "Akila, would your parents let us practice in your bonus room?"

"I can ask."

"Okay! Is everybody free this Saturday?" I asked.

"I need to check with my parents," Riley said. "They usually want me to help out at our booth at the farmer's market on Saturdays."

"Oh yeah," I said. The Jacobs family owns a free-range farm and huge organic garden. The farmer's market every Saturday is their busiest day, and as their only child, Riley is a big help to her parents in keeping things running smoothly. But hopefully she could find time to practice, too.

After a few more minutes of chatting and joking, the bell rang, and we all gathered our things and went to toss our trash. Lunch always went by so fast.

On our way out, Giana said, "So Riley and Akila will talk to their parents about Saturday, and Lay Lay and I will start thinking of a song next period during science. Harper, you start planning hair and makeup. And, Akila, we need bomb costumes. We can report back at lunch tomorrow to see where things are!"

"We got this!" I added. Though I knew Riley might need a little more convincing about leading a song. She always gave all of us so much support, but she sometimes had trouble accepting that she was good at things, too.

Giana and I walked to Mr. Lamar's science class in silence, bobbing and weaving between the other kids rushing down the hall, thinking over all we had to do.

Doing what I do every day, I know that pulling an act together is not easy, but we had to keep a winning attitude. Because, like Harper said, we have a part of history to preserve. Everybody had their assignments, and now it was just a matter of a few things falling into place. We had a long way to go over the next two weeks, but we have what it takes—the heart and the talent. Working together, we could accomplish something major.

I headed out of the school building with the other car riders and saw my cousin Tasha waiting for me. Tasha is a whole queen. She just graduated from the prestigious Samuelson School of Arts at Rieger College. She was a film major, and one day she wants to produce and direct her own feature films with diverse casts and crews. She's already done some cool indie projects. One of them won an award at a film festival hosted by her college.

I probably don't have to mention that my friends idolize everything she does, from her fashion sense to her edgy hair and makeup to her fiercely independent ideas about the world. When she decided to put us all to work helping out at

Hayes Theater, there was not an objection in the room. We couldn't wait for our first time to volunteer next to her. She is a total girl boss in the making.

My mom and dad travel a lot. Tasha looks out for me while they're away. Tasha's like a cool big sis. She has been there for me since forever—before all this viral stuff took off. She helps me get prepped for shows, interviews, and special appearances and helps me stay on point with all my social media.

"Hey, Lay Lay!" Tasha and I air-kissed on both cheeks like the French do. "How was your day, hun?"

I got settled in the car, and she pulled out of the line and into the winding parking lot toward the main road.

My school was about ten minutes from historic Woodlawn and the Hayes Theater. Tasha would spend a few hours working, and I would get a head start on my homework while scarfing down a veggie wrap and smoothie from Mr. Paul's shop across the square from the theater.

"It was good—wait, did you hear?" I asked, not wanting to miss a beat.

"Yeah, about Hayes Theater? Unfortunately, I did. My boss told me when I got in earlier today. Very sad. So much history. But it's just like greedy investors to come in and strip the life and culture from a place for some greasy dollars."

"Well, my friends and I have a plan to save it." I felt the shero in me rising.

"Oh, Lay Lay, you and your friends are so cute! Y'all are always up to something. What's your plan?"

"Well, today in school, our theater teacher, Ms. Duncan, announced our school talent show. She said the proceeds from the ticket sales would go to a charity nominated by the kids who enter the show."

"Oh, wow! That's big!"

"The winners also get to perform their winning act on TV!" I added.

"That's even bigger!" Tasha replied.

"Yeah, I know. Riley, Harper, Giana, Akila, and I thought we could nominate Hayes Theater. And if we win and get to perform on TV, we can use that opportunity to raise awareness for the Hayes, too."

"That is mighty generous of you, but I think you're forgetting one thing."

"I am?"

"Uh, yeah. When's the last time y'all performed in front of an audience?"

"It's been a minute, but we sort of have a group thing going on when we pretend to put on concerts at our sleepovers."

"Mm-hmm . . ." Tasha said. I don't know if she was buying it. "And how much money do you think you can raise from a talent show? Do you know how much is needed to keep Hayes Theater open?"

"No, but if we can convince Ms. Duncan and the rest of the school to choose Hayes Theater as the charity that receives the talent show proceeds, then whether we win or not, Hayes Theater gets some help, right?"

"Okay, I'm tracking with you," Tasha said. "Go on."

"But we really, really, really want to win so we

can get on News Channel 19 and tell everyone what's happening to historic Woodlawn. Then lots more money will come pouring in and we can save Hayes Theater!"

We pulled into the bumpy parking lot behind the theater. It had big dips and cracks in it. Where there was no cement or asphalt, gravel and grass took its place. The shrubs and other greenery around the building were overgrown, but it was nothing a light trim couldn't fix. The paint on the doors and shutters was chipped and faded, and the awning looked weathered. But at night Hayes Theater lit up like a Times Square Christmas tree, and all its splendor was on display. Finely dressed ushers in their maroon vests, crisp white shirts, and tuxedo pants waited in their spots to answer questions, hand out programs, and help you find your seat. Besides a few missing light bulbs, the majestic signage showed off the night's feature performance and beckoned theater lovers night after night.

Maybe we all had gotten used to its rough and patchy parts, just like you do with a favorite sweater. It's hard to see the wear and tear when you're so close to something. When something means so much, you sometimes see past its surface. Maybe this talent show was just the thing to cause us all to see both the beauty of the theater as well as its time for a much-needed makeover.

"Tasha?" I said once we were standing outside the car.

"Uh-huh?"

"Will you talk to your boss? Maybe the board of the theater can convince the developer to give us some time to raise money and prove that Hayes Theater is worth keeping open?"

"Lay Lay, I so love your spirit, girl. I love Hayes Theater, too. It's everything. I was feeling down about the news, but just for you I'm going to think positively about this, too. We got to try, right?"

"Yasss, Tasha!"

"All right. I'll talk to my boss."

"Yay! Thank you, Tasha!"

"Now, you go on upstairs to my office and get that homework done. Mr. Paul is sending someone over with your wrap and smoothie."

With that, we swung open both doors to the

theater and walked in at the same time like we owned the place—and this might actually be true one day. Don't sleep.

Later that night, after Tasha and I had dinner, I got to my room and messaged the girls to tell them Tasha had agreed to help. We talked more about our plan to use the News Channel 19 performance to raise awareness for the Hayes. The girls were still excited, but I could tell they were definitely feeling the pressure. Performing in front of our school was one thing. But performing on TV was something else.

"This is all you, Lay Lay," Giana texted. "We don't perform on TV every other day."

I decided not to push the issue anymore. I didn't want to put too much pressure on my friends. Performing is what I do all the time now. Them? Not so much. Though I knew they would come around, I needed to let them sleep on it.

"It's not all me. You're really amazing, too," I texted back. "We don't have to talk about it tonight. Let's get some rest and start fresh tomorrow. K?"

I signed off with a smiley-face emoji and some hearts. *They'll feel more excited about it tomorrow,* I told myself. *It will be a new day to dream big and focus on saving the Hayes.*

·✦· CHAPTER 4 ·✦·

THE NEXT DAY AT LUNCH, Riley reported that she wouldn't be able to rehearse with us unless she helped at the market with her parents first.

"You know what? It might be fun if we all come by and help," Harper cheerfully volunteered, saying out loud what we were all thinking.

"Actually," Giana said, "I think all our parents end up there at some point during the day. We can just walk from the market to Akila's house afterward. Then we can get our practice on."

She started a really bad imitation of pop lock-
ing, and then Riley started beatboxing and hyping
her up. We all crumbled over onto the table with
laughter. It was totally cringe. My friends are so
weird.

"Hey, so check it out," Akila said, grabbing her
sketchbook. "I've got some rough ideas for our
costumes."

"Oooooh . . ." we all said as we admired her
work.

"So I was thinking maybe we can all wear one
thing that's similar, like a jean jacket," she
explained.

"Oh, I like that a lot," Harper said.

"You know I love a jean jacket," I agreed.
"Though my favorite one is light blue, and I know
all of you have dark ones."

"Oh, we don't need to be too matchy-matchy,"
Akila replied. "I figure the jackets can match. But
then we can each choose a signature color for the
rest of the outfit."

"Yes!" Riley said. "I call yellow."

We all laughed. Yellow is Riley's favorite color,

and it's happy and sunny, just like her. It's one reason I call her Riley Smiley.

"Or we could get T-shirts made!" Riley added.

"We probably don't have time for that, right, Akila?" Giana said.

"Maybe. I could look into it and let you all know."

As we finished the last bites of our lunch, Riley went into her bag and pulled out a plastic container. "Hey, you guys, look what I brought." She opened the lid.

We oohed in unison again as the scent of oats, chocolate, and cherries wafted out. Anything Riley makes is amazing.

"I'm trying a new recipe for my go-to muffins. I figure it's a good idea to have some healthy, high-energy snacks on hand to keep us going."

Our mouths stuffed with sweet goodness, we all took a minute to respond.

"Great idea, Riles," Giana said between bites.

"Yes, very, very good," Akila said. She closed her eyes as she chewed Riley's treat.

"How in the world do you get vegan muffins to taste so good?" I asked.

"Well, I—"

"You know what?" I stopped her right there. "Don't tell me. Let me just enjoy them. Ignorance is bliss."

"Hey, what about those flyers?" Giana asked me. "Handing them out to everybody will give us more chances to talk about the history of Hayes Theater and what it means to our community. Lay Lay, you're on that, right?"

"Yes, I'm on it."

"Okay. Are you sure you can get it done?" Giana pressed. "You're always so busy."

"I got this," I replied. "As a matter of fact, I'll have a draft of it for you tomorrow."

"Okay, well . . ." Giana looked at me a little longer than necessary before she continued. "Let's email some ideas to Lay Lay about what we want to include on the flyer."

Yesterday, I had been worried about how we would pull off this talent show and save Hayes Theater. Today, after being with my friends at lunch, I was feeling better about it all. My friends were showing out with their ideas. People might think it's all about me, but wait till they see these queens in action. They aren't going to know what hit them. And for Hayes Theater, it's almost as good as saved. Our master plan was coming together.

Wednesdays are early-release days at school, so usually I go right home. I try to keep Wednesdays just for me, catching up on home-work, spending quality time with my girls, maybe a spa day—a little mani-pedi or facial— and catching up on my favorite, *The Charlene Wilson Show*. If Tasha could get me on this show, it would be on and poppin'. Ms. Charlene has every famous body and their mama on her show, and it's filmed nearby, too. I love the fast pace of my new life, but my mama is always teaching me about balance and self-care. You can't be your best for anybody else if you don't take care of yourself.

Unfortunately, my afternoon of me-time would have to wait because while my parents are out of town, I go with Tasha to the theater. And today I really had to study for tomorrow's big math test. I heard Mr. LaCourt takes time to write the tests himself and does not cut one corner, which means I've got to bring my A game.

Later, Giana, Riley, and I jumped on a group video chat to work on how to break up the verses for the song we were thinking of performing for the talent show. Riley told us about a spot in the song's hook that was giving her trouble, right before the bridge. "It's too high for me, I think. Can you do it, Giana?"

"Uh, that's a no from me, dawg," Giana said. "Maybe Akila can. Her voice is for sure higher than mine. What do you think, Lay?"

"Umm . . ." I tried to think. My brain was fried after studying for the math test. "Yeah, that sounds good."

"Really, Lay." Giana was not impressed. "Is this

what you're giving us tonight? We really need to pull together for this."

I felt bad. "I'm sorry, ladies. Okay, I'm here. Play the hook back again, Riley, and let's all sing along."

Riley played the last bit of the verse to lead us into the hook. Then we sang together. As we launched into the bridge, our voices screeched and cracked. We fell out in laughter.

"Yeah, that's high," I said. "Let's see how Akila sounds on it when we get together to practice Saturday."

"I think she'll do great," Giana said. "Now we just need to work on the transition between the bridge back to the hook and we'll be done."

"Sounds great! I'm so happy," Riley said. "Should we start from the top and see how it all flows?"

"I hate to do this," I interrupted. "But I'm going to have to ask for a part two. I have to get to bed so I can be up and ready for this super-early radio interview in the morning."

"Yeah, of course you do," Giana said. Was that a tone I was detecting?

"No worries," Riley said quickly. "We can keep working on it on Saturday."

"Lay Lay, you're going to work on those flyers tonight, right?"

"Uh, yeah." I really wasn't sure I could now, but I didn't want to flake out on the girls.

"I think we all emailed our ideas to you," Giana said.

"Right. Okay, I'm on it." If I couldn't get to the flyer tonight, I would knock it out in the morning since I had to be up with the roosters to do that radio spot.

"Well, if that's everything, I'm going to turn in, too," Riley said.

"Great! Sounds like a plan!" I said a bit too cheerfully, trying to balance out the negative vibes I was picking up from Giana. I made a mental note to ask Giana about her comments when I saw her tomorrow. I was worried she might be running out of patience with me and my new "Lay Lay world."

After our video chat, I brushed my teeth, washed my face, put on my pajamas, and got in bed. I didn't want to take the chance of being all draggy and boring during the interview, so I promised myself I would work on the flyer after the radio spot. As far as our performance for the talent show, I really did think the song we had chosen was the perfect way to represent me and my girls.

·✦· CHAPTER 5 ·✦·

WHEN LIFE SHOT OFF LIKE a rocket after my
video went viral, my parents knew some things
about my normal life would have to change. Thank
goodness, school wasn't one of them. Most kid performers like me end up leaving school and being
taught by tutors. I couldn't imagine doing that and
not seeing my friends every day!

It's tough trying to be a regular kid and a young
rap phenom, but the kids in my school aren't too
weird about it. Most of us went to elementary

school together. They get excited when they see me on TV or when I have a big concert over the weekend, but they just tell me they saw it and then we act normally. After my video blew up, the kids who didn't already know me—and a few who did— asked me for my autograph and to take pictures with them. That didn't last long, though. My teachers told me they expected some of this, and they suspected it would die down fast, too.

Woodlawn Middle is where I get to be myself. I can also count on my girls and, of course, Terrell, Reggie, and Brendon to keep me grounded. They won't ever let me get a big head about any of my success—which can be a good or bad thing, depending on the day.

Today was Thursday, and as soon as I saw my friends at our normal gathering spot, I felt the ground crumble beneath me. I did not have the draft of the flyer ready. My morning had been such a rush. The DJ was late for the radio spot, and I went on later than we had planned. Instead of having an hour, I had less than thirty minutes to get from the radio station to school on time.

I could feel Giana reading me as I walked up to them: "You forgot it, didn't you?"

"I really tried to get it done, but I ran out of time. The DJ was late to the station, and then I had to squeeze in a couple of minutes to study for Mr. LaCourt's math test. Gi, I really tried."

"Well, at least it was only a draft, right, Giana?" Harper said, trying to keep things light.

"I guess so," Giana said, turning away from me.

I felt the cold shoulder I knew she wanted me to feel. I had let my friends down.

"Yeah, it will be fine, Lay," Riley said. "Could you have a draft to show us at rehearsal on Saturday?"

"Mm-hmm." I didn't want my words to betray me again, but I would do everything I could to make it up.

"Okay, see?" Riley said. "Easy as pie."

I wasn't too sure of that. Giana's patience seemed to be wearing thin with me. I tried to change the subject. "So Tasha found out from her boss that the Hayes is set to host its last show in four weeks. The talent show is in two weeks . . ."

"Which means the TV performance is right before the theater's last show ever!" Harper said, finishing my thought.

"Oh no! This means we have to win," Akila said. "There's no room for mistakes. We've got to nail each step in our plan."

"That goes for making sure we have those flyers ready for next week, Lay Lay," Giana added.

"And we can't forget the essay," Riley reminded us.

"Right," Harper said. "It's due tomorrow. I have all your ideas added in. I'll send a copy by email tonight. You can let me know if it's all good."

"Perfect," Giana said. "Hayes Theater has to be the charity that wins the school's vote so it gets all the proceeds from the talent show."

"And if we win the talent show, that'll be icing on the cake," Harper said. "That News Channel 19 appearance will help us make the whole town aware that the theater will be torn down if people don't step up to save it."

"Hey, we can do this. Okay?" Riley had me doing a double take. She sounded like me with a little

Giana mixed in. "We have a good plan. Let's stick to it. All hands in. Say 'Winners!' on five."

One at a time, a little scared by Riley's sudden take-charge attitude, we stacked our hands one on top of another. We counted to five in unison and shouted, "Winners!"

The bell rang, and we scattered to our classes.

Mr. LaCourt's math test was brutal. I may have been able to pull off a C, but it was hard to tell. I saw Akila walking up ahead toward the musical theater room.

"Hey, Akila, wait up." Judging by her face, I could almost predict her answer to my next question: "How did you do?"

"Oh, not so good."

"Aw, yeah. Me neither."

"I don't even know why I try."

"Aw, Akila, don't say that."

It wasn't like my friend to be down on herself.

Akila was usually all confidence all the time.

"No, really, Lay. It seems like things just keep getting harder. I studied, but when I got to the test, I didn't recognize anything."

"It wasn't just you. I was confused, too. Don't let Mr. LaCourt get to you. He thinks he's 'challenging' us."

"Well, I think he wants me to fail."

"Oh, don't say that. You probably did better than you think."

"No, I'm pretty sure I bombed it."

"Don't be too hard on yourself, Kee. You're so smart, and you work hard at everything you do."

"Yeah, well, try telling that to my dad."

"I would if I wasn't scared of him."

She laughed at that, and I did, too. Akila's dad was great, but he could be intense. I hoped that she passed Mr. LaCourt's test more than I hoped it for myself. My friend really did deserve everything.

It seemed like it took forever to get to Friday. Harper managed to get all our ideas into the one-page essay, and we signed up for the talent show. While that was one really good thing, the math test and all the running around I'd been doing had me feeling kind of blah. So instead of jumping right into my homework after school like I do most days—you know, get the hard stuff done first—I needed to hit refresh on my mood. I thought, what better way was there for me to get a shot of happy than to see if my girls were down for a last-minute dance party sleepover. As soon as I hit send on the invite, my notifications were popping off with yeses all around. *Did they ask their parents that fast?* Oh well, that's none of my business!

I stepped into the auditorium, where Tasha was working. I hoped she'd be cool with our spontaneous slumber party. I heard her talking with a man. It sounded like he was the producer for a play that was coming to town.

"So, Mr. Johnson, your show will be the last play at the Hayes before we close our doors."

"That's too bad. This place has special meaning

to some of our cast and crew. You know this was the first theater in this area that began booking Black performers. It's been a special place for a lot of Black audiences, too. We'll fill this place up and give it a great send-off."

"That sounds like just what we need," Tasha replied.

Tasha turned and spotted me in the back of the theater. "Hey, Lay Lay. What's up, girl?"

"Wow, is that true about Hayes Theater?" I asked her.

Tasha nodded. "This place is legendary. I only wish more people realized. But you and your friends are trying to help, and that means a lot, Lay Lay."

"We aren't just trying to help—we're so gonna do it!" I replied. "And speaking of my friends . . ."

I decided to say it superfast so my question would speed past her better sense and get right to her reply. "Can the girls come over and spend the night?"

Tasha laughed. "I'm too tired to go back and forth with you over it, so yes, that's fine."

It worked! I was pumped. Just as I was about to say something, my stomach growled so loud I thought Tasha had said something!

"Lay Lay, have you eaten?"

Slightly embarrassed, I made a fake ashamed face.

"Honey, you cannot do that to yourself. Let's go up to my office. I have something special waiting for you."

"Ooh, Tasha! For real!" I was giddy all over again. It was about to be over—O-V-E-R—if she'd stopped at my favorite burger place and gotten the smoked portobello mushroom burger and sweet potato waffle fries.

We got up to her office, and when I saw that brown bag with red letters, I knew.

"Tasha! Girl, you did not. You are looking out!"

I grabbed the bag, and I did not pass go or collect $200. I went straight to the nearest seat and dug in.

"Ah, this is so good! Fam. And you got me a gingerberry kombucha, too?" I put on my best about-to-ugly-cry face. "Girl, I could cry."

"Ew, stop talking with your mouth full. And don't eat too fast. I don't want you getting heartburn."

Tasha had helped raise my happy level ten notches. Then the slumber party tonight was sure to send it through the roof. I couldn't wait to get home.

·◆· CHAPTER 6 ·◆·

EVERYTHING WAS SET. TASHA AND I had stopped by the grocery store to get veggie wraps and frozen fruit, yogurt, and juice to make smoothies. We also ordered pizza and two-liters. Oh, and popcorn—lots of popcorn.

The family room furniture was pushed to the walls, and piles of pillows, throws, and comfy blankets covered the floor. I looked around the room to see what was missing. *Maybe another body pillow?* Just as I was about to run down the hall to the linen closet, the doorbell rang. It was seven o'clock on the dot.

"I got it!" I yelled to Tasha. Knowing her, she was already in her pj's and in bed with her blanket pulled up to her neck.

"Okay, y'all have fun," Tasha said. "I'm in here if you need anything."

"Okay!" I yelled back as I yanked the door open. "Harper! Riley!" I waved out the door to Riley's mom as she pulled away.

We kiss-kissed like Tasha and I do, and they piled into the foyer with all their junk.

"Y'all are just staying the night, right?"

"Yeah, but you know, it's girls' night," Harper said with a sly smile. "I brought over all kinds of stuff for mani-pedis, facials, makeovers . . . Eee! This is going to be so much fun."

"Well, I just brought more treats for us to munch on," said Riley.

"Okay," I said. "Get in here. I set up everything in the family room."

The doorbell rang two more times, and our girl squad of five was complete.

"Let's get this party started!" Giana shouted.

Harper put on some music, and we started bouncing and bobbing to the heavy bass all barefoot and hair flying over every inch of the room. This was just what we needed.

"Hey." Riley elbowed me as the next song started. "Let's go get those smoothies going."

Harper followed behind us, singing with a microphone that was really a hairbrush. She was putting on a show. Akila laughed at the spectacle, while Giana played the instrumental solo with her air guitar.

We pulled out all the fixings for the smoothies. Smoothies were a whole thing in my house, so we had a hand blender, a single-cup blender, and a regular one, too. We each came up with our own delicious blend. It got quiet in the kitchen since no one was running the DJ booth.

"Mmm." Akila put a finger up while she swallowed her last bit of strawberry acai smoothie. "I made some changes to our look for the talent show. Want to see?"

"Ooh yeah," Riley said.

Akila pulled out a notebook full of her designs.

"Okay, so here's what I've got," Akila said. "So everyone has a signature color, right? And we're each wearing a jean jacket, but I think we need something more. I can make some shiny star patches in the different colors, and we can add them to our jackets or pants if we want!"

"Oh, that sounds great, Kee," I said.

"I love it," Riley said, bobbing her head. "And I already claimed yellow."

"I have all the supplies at home," Akila continued. "So when you come over tomorrow, we can get the patches done."

"That's perfect," Giana said. "I want turquoise to match my glasses. And Lay Lay should be hot pink— she looks amazing in it."

"Thanks, Gigi," I said. Leave it to my bestie to remember pink was one of my favorite colors.

"I'm so glad you all like it," Akila said. She let out a breath of relief. I wondered how long she had obsessed over it.

"It's amazing," Harper agreed. "And you should be purple, Akila. I know you love it. That means I should do something bright and fresh, like lime green or orange. Oh! I am so going with orange so I can wear my new hair bow!"

"Well, now that that's decided, should we go watch a movie?" Riley asked.

"Yes, let's!" Harper led the way back into the family room. I grabbed a couple big bowls and two big bags of kettle corn and followed right behind.

Giana got the movie cued, and we settled in on our big pillows and wrapped ourselves in blankets.

"This movie has some choreo in it that I think will be easy for us to learn for the talent show," Akila said as she stretched out on her tummy.

Twenty minutes into the movie, Tasha appeared in the doorway of the family room. She was motioning for me to come over to her.

"Hey, Lay Lay, I'm so sorry," she said in a hushed tone as she walked me to the kitchen.

"What's going on?"

"I got a call from the Sun Times, and they want to interview you for a national feature they're doing on young artists and how they're balancing real life with fame."

"Oh, that's what's up! Tell them yes."

"Hey, Lay Lay!" Giana yelled from the family room. "Hurry up. It's getting to the good part."

"Okay! I'm coming!" I started to walk back to the family room.

"No, Lay Lay. The reporter is on the phone now. They're working on a really tight deadline."

"Oh no."

"Yeah, I know. I really do think you should do it. This is not an everyday opportunity."

"Ugh! What do I tell my friends?"

"They'll be fine. The interview shouldn't take that long."

"Okay. Can you tell the girls for me? I'll run up real quick and take the call in my room."

What I thought was going to be a twenty- or thirty-minute interview turned into almost two hours. That reporter wouldn't stop talking. I ran downstairs hoping the girls were still lit. Not even. They were all knocked out! Or so I thought.

When I tried to quietly slip back into my blanket burrito, I caught Giana's eyes from across the room. She didn't need to say a word. I knew right then; I had really messed up. She turned her back to me and did not respond when I whispered her name a few times.

Rather than falling asleep exhausted from laughter and eating too much, I drifted to sleep with my thoughts on how I had let down my friends once again.

The next morning, I woke up with a foot in my face and a hand on my foot. I blinked a few times, and the fogginess started to go away. I remembered that I had messed up, and Giana probably wasn't speaking to me.

"Girls! Wake up!" Tasha called from the kitchen. "We gotta get you over to the farmer's market in an hour."

We all slowly rose and dragged ourselves upstairs to my room.

"Who's getting in the shower first?" Giana asked.

"Me," answered Akila. "I'll be quick."

One at a time, we each got into the shower, came out, got dressed, went downstairs, and grabbed one of Riley's amazing muffins and a juice box. We were efficient, like an assembly line, and made it to the car in under an hour.

Tasha dropped us all off at the farmer's market. From the entrance, I could see the long line in front of the Jacobs Family Farm booth. Riley's mom and dad were counting up and cashing out orders as quickly as they could. It was clear they needed us.

Riley didn't hesitate. She sprang right into action. Every few seconds she would appear in front of one of us and tell us what we needed to do.

Zip. Zip!

"Giana, please grab some baskets and walk through the booth to see if anyone has questions. Here's a price sheet."

"Roger that!" Giana answered.

Zip. Zip!

"Akila, if you wouldn't mind, please go stand by the meat and dairy cooler to help my dad get people the cuts of meat they need."

"Okay, I can do that."

Zip. Zip!

"Harper and Lay Lay, can you help bag produce at the checkout table? Pretty please?"

"Got it!" we said at the same time.

"Okay, and I'll go make sure all the produce has been put out."

This was a whole new Riley for me—still sweet but also kind of a boss. I liked it!

Riley's parents were nice. They both looked just like her—ginger-haired, fair skin, and freckles. They were such a cute family!

After a few hours, things started to slow down.

"You girls swooped in right on time," Riley's dad said.

"Oh my gosh, yes, thank you all so much!" Riley's mom agreed.

"Mom, do you think it will be okay if we head over to Akila's for rehearsal now?"

Looking at Riley's dad for confirmation, she said,

"That should be fine. I'll pick you up around five? Is that good?"

We all looked at one another, nodding.

"Great. Bye, Mom. Thanks!"

We raced off to Akila's.

Two hours into our rehearsal, things were going really well.

"This is looking fine, y'all," I said. "And you sound amazing, Riley."

Riley smiled shyly. "Thanks, Lay Lay."

"Let's go over the choreo from the movie one more time," Akila suggested. "We were so close that last time."

"What was the last step again?" I asked. I wanted to be sure I nailed it.

"Well, if you'd actually watched the movie with us, you'd know," Giana said.

Ouch. That hurt. But at least Gi was speaking to me again!

"Here, Lay Lay, I'll show you," Akila jumped in quickly. Then she demonstrated the move one more time. It looked amazing—Akila's gymnastic skills make her an incredible dancer.

We ran through the act again and left off feeling pretty confident. *Phew!* All we needed was a group name. But after staying up late last night, we just didn't have the juice to keep going.

We made plans for another rehearsal—same time, same place next week. I headed home feeling great about the act but less great about me and Gi. I hoped she'd come around soon.

·✦· CHAPTER 7 ·✦·

IN THEATER CLASS ON MONDAY, Ms. Duncan skipped her normal schedule and gave us the whole period to work in our groups. With the talent show happening in a little over a week, we needed the time. My friends and I gathered in our favorite corner.

"So where are we after rehearsal Saturday?" Giana started us off. "Costumes?"

"Check," Akila answered. "Everybody has jean jackets to wear, right? And we each picked a signature color, so we're good. I'll finish making some fun patches in each color that we can add on, and we'll be all good."

"All right. Song and choreo?"

"We're doing great on both, I think," Riley said.

"Me too," Harper said. "Moving, singing, and styling all at the same time is not easy."

"Hair and makeup?"

"I tried a couple looks on everybody during the movie, except for Lay Lay," Harper said. "I'll get you later, girl. No worries!"

I just knew I would get a comment from Giana. But she didn't say anything. She didn't even look at me. *Ugh!* I guess it was back to the silent treatment. Then I remembered—*the flyers!*

"And the flyers?" Giana must have read my thoughts and knew.

"Uh, yeah, about the flyers . . ." I needed to be bailed out again, but no one said anything to help. "I, uh . . . I haven't gotten to them yet."

"Lay Lay, really?" Giana said. "Wednesday is the vote! If we don't have those flyers tomorrow, we'll miss the chance to make sure everybody knows about Hayes Theater. Are you even with us in this, or is this really all about you, like everybody is saying?"

Whoa. There were the words that matched the looks I'd been getting. I was speechless.

Harper jumped in. "Don't say it like that, Giana," she said. "It's more like we know you have a busy life and everything, but, like, you're our friend, too . . ."

"Yeah, we love you, Lay, but you're kind of letting us down," Riley said.

"I didn't mean what I said like that," Giana backtracked. "I guess I wish you were really, you know, here with us. Everybody loves you, Lay Lay. And I don't blame them."

"This one kid came up to me and asked if you were going to perform at the talent show and if I was going to be your backup dancer," Akila said.

"Yeah, same," Harper said.

"And I wish that you'd just do what you say you'll do so I don't have to feel like maybe everybody is right. Like you're this big star and we're not all that important anymore." Giana was looking down now, and I knew she was trying hard not to cry.

"Oh, you guys! I feel terrible! I'm trying hard to balance my life as That Girl Lay Lay and still be your friend, and I am not doing a good job at all. I'm really, really sorry."

"Giana is right, Lay Lay," Riley said. "It's been a little rough, but we forgive you. You know you always have us."

"Aw, thank you, Riley Smiley," I said.

Riley smiled back, showing her big dimples.

"We love being your friends—superstar rapper or not," Harper said.

"Yeah, I just need to be better at coming through for y'all," I admitted. "'Cause with y'all, I am not a solo act. It's us five until we die. And I know this fact: If everyone thought I was good by myself, they are going to pass out when they see us all strutting across that stage—together!"

"Okay!" Giana said. I hoped she had accepted my apology.

"And that's that on that!" Harper said. Her silky-straight ponytail wagged as she rolled her neck and snapped.

"Period!" we all yelled together before we fell out laughing.

"Okay, y'all, for real. Anyone think of any good names since yesterday?" Giana brought us back to order. "Boo Crew is out."

"What? Why?" Riley whined.

"C'mon, Riley," Giana said. "Boo Crew, really?"

We laughed. It was a little cringy.

"I kind of like Lit Chicks," Harper said. "It sounds like us."

"Yeah, but it's not the one," Akila replied. "You know what I mean?"

"It kind of sounds like a middle-aged woman's book club, if you ask me," Giana said. And she would know. She's the most bookish of us all.

"Well, I hate to be the spoiler here, but the bell is about to ring," Akila said.

And the bell did ring.

I closed my notebook and headed toward the

door, thoughts still going. We were still a girl group of five with no name. Oh well.

"So, Lay Lay, are you coming to perform at the talent show as a featured artist? Or are you too good for us?" Reggie spotted me walking across the lunchroom to meet my friends at our table. *Ugh, why doesn't he get a life on this sweet Tuesday morning?*

He was standing at the front of his table with his little crew behind him. He said what he said loud enough for the kids around us to hear his nonsense.

"Reggie, what are you talking about?"

"You heard me. You've been on the come-up lately. I just want to know if your homies here will get an exclusive show."

"Reggie, we've been through this already. Me *and* my girls are coming to *compete* in the talent show."

"Yeah, and we're bringing that heat," Giana said,

"and your boys better watch out." We had time today.

"Oh, okay, I see how it is. I guess you realized you couldn't take us down by yourself, then, huh, Lay Lay?"

Some of the kids chuckled a little bit. Emily was turned all the way around in her seat cheesing at me. I guess she was waiting for my comeback. I looked at her like "Ma'am, can I help you?" She turned back around so fast.

"Naw, bruh, you trippin'," I said, turning back to Reggie. "I would have no problem handling y'all on my own. Matter of fact, I can rap circles around you and your crew by myself."

"Oh, okay. I see."

"Oh, you're about to see for real. Somebody give me a beat. I'll spit over anything."

Terrell was game, so he started beatboxing like those old-school emcees.

"Okay, Terrell. I see you." I was feeling the groove. I grabbed my lip gloss and slid it on while I got my head together.

My girls came around and were hyping me up:

"Yeah, yeah, yeah! Go, Lay Lay! Go, Lay Lay!"

"Okay, okay, okay . . ." I was getting in the zone. Then I let loose. I started spitting fire like crazy, busting rhymes left and right about Hayes Theater. I was so fired up I kept going on and on about how the Hayes was a piece of history and we had to save it.

IT'S YA GIRL LAY, AND I'M HERE TO SLAY

I'M ABOUT TO RHYME AND MAKE Y'ALL SWAY

MY GIRLS ARE FLY, AND WE IN THE HOUSE—AYE!

GOT A TALENT SHOW TO KILL, BUT IT AIN'T ABOUT LAY!

HAYES THEATER IS OUR CAUSE; WE AIN'T LETTING UP

THEY'RE TRYING TO TEAR IT DOWN; THAT AIN'T WHAT'S UP

IT'S A PIECE OF HISTORY

IT AIN'T A MYSTERY

WE GOTTA SAVE OUR TOWN

FROM THIS MISERY

IF YOU KNOW WHAT'S UP, THEN YOU ON THE BOAT

IF YOU'RE ROCKING WITH US, THEN YOU ROCK THE VOTE!

IF YOU KNOW WHAT'S GOOD, THEN YOU HEARD THE WORD

I'M THAT GIRL LAY FROM WOODLAWN IN THE BURBS

"Ohhhhh!" Everybody was screaming and yelling all over the lunchroom. "Yo, Lay Lay just killed that!"

I heard kids starting to talk about the theater. Suddenly there was a lot of chatter about voting for the Hayes. That was the most important part. I hadn't planned it, but this little cameo may have done a better job than those flyers would have done if I didn't keep forgetting about them.

"You satisfied, Reggie?"

"I mean, you nice or whatever." Reggie was sounding real humble. "But we knew that. Don't let us catch your girls slipping. We're coming for that top spot."

"It's not all about winning, Reggie. We've got a piece of history to save."

Things fizzled with Reggie, and we went to our separate corners. Me to my friends, and he to his. As we walked to our table, kids were coming over and telling me how great my freestyle was. A lot of them were saying they were going to vote for Hayes Theater to be the recipient of the talent show funds.

"Lay Lay, that was awesome!" Harper said.

"Yeah, everybody loved it," Riley said.

"And everybody's talking about Hayes Theater," Akila said. "Rapping about Hayes Theater might have been the magic we needed to get people to vote for it tomorrow."

I looked at Giana, hoping all was forgiven, though I still had not done those flyers!

"That was really cool, Lay Lay," she said with a tight smile. Nope, I still had more making up to do.

On Wednesday, Tasha came to pick me up from school. When I got in the car, she was on the phone in an intense conversation with somebody.

"He can't do that!" Tasha gasped. "That's not right!"

The other person said something, but I don't think Tasha could hear. Her emotions were loud.

"What are we supposed to do now?"

The other person said something again.

"Well, we won't give up." Tasha ended the call.

"What's going on?" I asked.

"That was my boss, and he was just telling me that the board met with the real estate developer. They were hoping to get more time. Instead, the developer says he has to move up the deadline by one week to match the schedule of the construction company he hired for the teardown. If we don't come up with the money to refurbish the theater by then, it has to go."

"Oh no, this is terrible!" I moaned.

"I know, Lay. What are we going to do?"

"I was feeling so hopeful. We just voted at school for the theater to be our charity for the talent show! But the important part of this whole thing was the TV performance a week later."

I knew that if we didn't get on News Channel 19, we'd never get the whole community involved. Ms. Duncan told us how much had been raised so far from ticket sales, and it just wasn't enough. That TV appearance would have to take us over the top.

"Well, we can't give up," I said. "There's got to be another way."

"I don't know, Lay. But it's not looking good, Tasha said quietly. "I know you and your friends are working hard, but don't get your hopes up."

·✦· CHAPTER 8 ·✦·

THE NEXT FEW DAYS WENT quickly. We had the same plans for this Saturday, but after the news about the theater and the talent show ticket sales, we were feeling kind of deflated. It felt like things were starting to unravel. Akila couldn't be with us when we helped out at the Jacobs Family Farm booth. She had sprained her ankle after a hard fall at her gymnastics meet earlier in the week. She needed to stick to just the essentials, like school, for the next few days until she went to see the doctor again.

"Are you worried about missing gymnastics training?" I asked her when we got to her house that afternoon for our rehearsal.

She sat in one of the recliners in her living room with her ankle raised and wrapped. "No, I guess not. I think I'm more worried about not being able to perform with you all."

"Aw, Akila . . ." Riley stood behind Akila's chair and smoothed over Akila's pulled-back ponytail. Riley was the sweetest. "You don't need to think about that now. You're still part of the group."

"Maybe we can make you a blinged-out chair to sit in onstage," Harper said, jumping up as if she was about to craft the chair right there. "You might not be able to dance, but your vocals are still on point."

"That's a thought," Giana said. "What do you want to do, Akila?"

"Really, though, she doesn't have to make a decision today. Right, Akila?" Riley interrupted. "She goes to see the doctor again on Tuesday, and the talent show isn't till Friday. We have a little time. Let's take some of the pressure off and just practice for now." She gave Akila a quick squeeze and came to sit down with the rest of us on the carpet.

"You're right, Ms. Riley," I said as Riley sat. "Let's focus on getting these lyrics, the last bit of choreo, and—

"Okay. I'm sorry, but I've been trying to get us to focus this whole time," Giana said. "And now just 'cause you're saying it, Lay Lay, 'we all need to focus.'" She finished her statement with air quotes.

Riley looked down. Harper's head swiveled like she was watching tennis. Akila looked right at me with that "ah, that hurts" kind of face.

I had just been ambushed. I had no words. "What are you talking about, Giana?"

"Are you serious, Lay Lay? You've been half here with us and half in your other life, doing radio and news interviews every time we try to get this performance together. It's not us who need to focus—it's you!"

Oh no!

"Giana, I'm doing the best I can. Between school, trying to be there for you guys, Hayes Theater, and this talent show . . . it's all too much."

"So, what, we're too much now?"

That was a gut punch.

"No, Giana, that's not what I mean at all," I said. "I'm sorry if you feel that I'm not contributing to this performance like the rest of you are. This is the last thing I ever wanted to happen."

My literal nightmare was playing out right here in real life. This was bad.

"I don't know about that," Giana replied. "I bet it would be so much easier if you just raised money for Hayes Theater and did the talent show on your own. You've got your own songs, your own choreo, and outfits for days."

"Giana, that is not true at all!" I protested. "I'm trying to say sorry, but you won't let it go."

"Am I the only one who sees that Lay Lay isn't really here with us, that she's acting like she could do this all better without us?"

"Giana, Lay Lay, you need to stop right now," Akila said, standing up even with her injured foot.

"We are not going to do this. We've been friends for too long."

"She just thinks she's all that, and I'm tired of always being seen as one of her groupies," Giana said. "I'm good at stuff, too."

Then she fell apart into tears.

I went over to hug her, and I started crying, too. Then Akila came over and started crying, then Riley, and even happy Harper. We just hugged one another and cried.

Finally, we got our composure back.

"I never wanted things to be this way, Giana," I said. "I could tell that something was going on between us, but with everything else happening, I never found the time to ask you how you were doing. You are my sister from another mister. I could never see you—or any of the girls—as a backup to anything. Forget what everybody else thinks. You are a headliner and so good at everything you do."

"I *am* pretty awesome." Giana was starting to perk up. "I don't know what got into me, but I guess seeing all these great things happen for you hasn't been as easy for me as I wanted it to be. It used to be just us—you, me, and Akila. Then, when Riley and Harper came along, we were as tight as ever. But now hearing from the kids at school that I should be your backup really got me. The real truth is, I was feeling left out. But the even realer truth is that I am so glad all these things are happening for you, Lay Lay."

"Aw, Giana." We hugged again. "You don't know how much I needed to hear you say that. I've been so worried you would feel that I wasn't the same Lay Lay anymore."

"Lay Lay, I know you better than anybody," Giana said. "I know you love the spotlight and chasing your dreams. But don't forget us."

"I could never," I said. I was a little sad that Giana would even think I would forget her or any of my friends. I had some reevaluating to do.

"So are we doing this show and saving Hayes Theater or not?" Harper's sharp question brought us back to reality.

"Yes!" we all said together, laughing off the tension of the last few minutes.

"And, um, what are we going to call ourselves?" I asked. "'Cause the talent show is on Friday, as in six-days-from-now Friday."

"The Five Hearts?" Riley blurted out.

"No!" the rest of us said in unison.

·◆·: CHAPTER 9 ·◆·:

MONDAY MORNING HIT HARD, ESPECIALLY after that blowout we had on Saturday. I was still feeling pretty down about the Hayes. I was trying to stay positive, but would it even matter if we did the talent show? I couldn't let myself think like that. This was the week of the performance. I had to show the girls that I would be there for them no matter what.

A call came in on our landline before school. It was a producer from *The Charlene Wilson Show*. They wanted to book me for an interview and a performance. My jaw hit the floor as Tasha told me the news.

Charlene Wilson has the biggest daytime talk show ever. Millions of people around the world watch her. She books the most famous guests, and she never really has newcomers like me. This was an amazing opportunity. I couldn't believe it.

"There's good news and bad news, Lay Lay," Tasha told me once she got off the phone.

"Okay! What's the good news?" I said, spinning around. I really was that giddy.

"Her show is filmed about an hour from here."

"Right. That's great!" I knew that part. "What's the bad news?"

"She just had a spot open up due to another artist canceling—but it's on the same day as your school's talent show."

"What? Tasha, you can't be serious? How am I supposed to do both?"

"Well, let's think this through 'cause you are going to do *Charlene Wilson*."

"Tasha, this is all I've been dreaming of, but I can't let my girls down."

"I know, Lay Lay. And if there's any chance of saving Hayes Theater, you've got to do the talent show, too. But this is Charlene Wilson we're talking about. This is hard."

"Well, what time is the taping?"

"They want you there at three p.m."

"Oh, that should give me plenty of time. The talent show isn't until seven. But then we need to be there at six to get set up and do a sound check . . ." I mumbled that last part to myself. I was feeling time beginning to crunch in on me again. I really hoped I could do both shows.

"Not so fast, Lay Lay. You know how these things go. You get there at three, sign in, and end up having to do lots of waiting. There's a run-through, and then finally your real segment with Charlene. It could all take several hours."

"I think I can make it." I was determined to.

Tasha went on. "Then you have to factor in the drive time. Her studio is about an hour away from your school on a good day."

"First of all, it's yes to Charlene Wilson," I said, not willing to miss this once-in-a-lifetime opportunity. "And maybe I can make a plug for Hayes Theater while I'm on the show!"

"Oh, that would be really great. I wonder . . ." Tasha took a long pause. "I wonder if we could get Charlene Wilson to help the cause, too."

"Hmm . . . I think it's worth a try," I said. "We've gotta try."

It was just simple time management, right?

"I know this will work," I said confidently. "I'll do *The Charlene Wilson Show* and still make it to perform with the girls. I don't believe that one good thing has to take away another good thing. I can have it all."

"Okay, Lay Lay," Tasha said, shaking her head at my optimism. Maybe she was buying what I was selling. "I'll do my best to help make it all happen but just let the girls know. You don't want them to be taken by surprise if you're late or can't make it at all."

"Are you kidding me? How is that supposed to work, Lay Lay? You are not a time bender. This is exactly what I was talking about the other day." Giana was fuming after I told the girls about *The Charlene Wilson Show*.

I'd been a little scared this would happen. I didn't want Giana to blow up at me again, but I knew I could make it work. I *had* to make it work—for my friends *and* for Hayes Theater.

Riley was supportive.

"I'm super excited for you, Lay Lay," she said. "Honestly, Charlene Wilson?! It's like all your dreams are coming true!"

"This is pretty freaking amazing, if you ask me," Harper added. "I feel like it's me going on that show!"

Giana spoke up again.

"If it were on any other day than this Friday, the same day as the talent show, I'd be turning flips for you. Lay Lay, you're my whole BFF. But, like, how is it all supposed to work? You can't be everywhere at once."

"Hold on, Giana," Akila said, playing negotiator

again. "If Lay Lay says she can make it all work, we have to trust her. She's our friend."

"Okay, put it to me straight, Lay Lay," Giana said. "If you look me in my eyes and tell me right now that you really think you can make it back to the school on time to perform with us, you won't hear a peep from me about it again."

I didn't answer her right away. I needed a minute to think and to cool down.

We finished going through the lunch line and sat down together with our food. I took a deep breath.

"I don't know how I'll make it work, but I know I have to try," I said honestly. "After talking things through with Tasha, I realize this isn't just about my dream. This may actually be our last chance to save Hayes Theater."

"What do you mean, Lay Lay?" Riley asked.

"Tasha and I were thinking I could make a plug for the theater on Ms. Charlene's show, and maybe we could get her support, too."

"Wow. That's a great idea!" Harper said.

"I promise I am not trying to be all over the place, and I definitely don't want to let you down,"

I told Giana. Couldn't she see that? "I also don't think I should have to choose between the good things in life. And this is all just too good. I love y'all, I love the history of our city, and I am getting to go on this amazing show. It's all yeses for me."

Giana crossed her arms and sat back in her seat. "I'm not saying you shouldn't do it, Lay. I'd just like to see how you're going to make all this happen."

"What if we come up with a plan B?" Harper suggested. "Akila's ankle is iffy at this point. Lay Lay may be late or not show up at all . . ."

"I don't know about that, Harper," Riley said slowly. "Do you think we can pull it off without Lay Lay and Akila?"

"Don't count me out just yet," Akila said.

"And, y'all, I'm sitting right here," I said, feeling defensive. "Y'all are not about to plan for failure. We got this. You hear me?"

"Okay, Lay Lay," Giana said, sighing. "You better not stand us up."

"Girl, I got y'all," I promised.

Giana is my homie, but she can be so dramatic sometimes. There was a whole lot going on, and I

could understand why she was getting nervous—
we all were. But we didn't have time for the drama.
This last-minute opportunity to appear on *The
Charlene Wilson Show* came at just the right time for a
reason. No way was I going to pass it up. I hoped
that with the rest of the group's optimism, Giana
would see this would all work out better than fine.

·✦· CHAPTER 10 ·✦·

I WOKE UP FRIDAY MORNING on cloud nine. I knew today would be tough, but it would also be my chance to live out everything I had dreamed all in one day—an international TV appearance, a bomb performance later with my girls, and saving Hayes Theater. I mean, what could be better?

Between Tasha and the girls, we had planned everything out to a T. We were going to head to Charlene Wilson's TV studio early to sign papers and get my crew set up for a little behind-the-scenes footage and to help with hair and makeup touch-ups. The girls would head over to the school a little before six to get checked in and look over their costumes. If I was there in time, I'd join for the sound check. If not, they would handle it without me.

Our costumes were simple so we could easily look like a group—and cute, 'cause, well, that's just what we do. Simple jean jackets with our signature color underneath. Akila had envisioned a 1990s hip-hop girl aesthetic to go with the song we chose. Not too much to fuss over.

Tasha would pick me up from school after lunch so I had time to get ready before she drove me to Charlene Wilson's set. As soon as the director called "cut" on my segment with Charlene, Tasha and I would jump in her car and get over to the school as fast as we could for the talent show. The plan was airtight.

The girls and I had called an emergency rehearsal last night while Akila was at another doctor's appointment. Akila seemed pretty sure the doctor would tell her she couldn't perform the next day.

Harper's idea of a chair onstage seemed to be the best thing. We tried to make Akila see it as a total diva move when we told her over the phone, but it didn't work. The perfectionist she is, she was pretty sad about having to sit it out.

The rest of us were able to focus on hammering out the final harmonies. We did a couple perfect run-throughs of the song. Everything was set.

I was just getting out of my preshow bubble bath when Tasha knocked on the door. "Lay Lay, hun, it's time to come out. We gotta get moving and get you glammed up, girl."

"Okay, I'm almost done," I hollered from my side of the door.

When I got out of the bathroom, Tasha already had things working. When it came to the drip needed to satisfy an audience, Tasha played zero games. I loved to see her do what she loves.

Tasha picked out a fluffy pink skirt and a matching shirt to go with my favorite blinged-out jean jacket. Next, she parted my hair down the middle and fixed it in two cute buns. Then she, of course, laid my edges. I was looking so fly.

Watching the clock is the worst thing you can do when you're waiting, but it was taking forever to be called in to film my segment with Ms. Charlene. We'd been at the studio since three o'clock, and it was now four thirty. Even though Tasha told me TV show recordings sometimes go like this, I didn't want to believe her. I was beginning to doubt I was going to be able to keep my word to Giana and the girls.

Just then, one of the producers called us in. It was finally time for my segment with Charlene Wilson! I had rehearsed with a stand-in, but this was the real deal. I was about to be sitting right across from the host of the biggest daytime TV talk show. One crew member was entertaining the audience while another walked me over to my place on set. The theme music went up in the house, and Charlene Wilson, looking ever so diva, came out to roaring applause. She stopped on her mark a few feet away from where I sat and started her introduction.

"Hey, everybody! My next guest is someone you may have seen heating up the social media scene. After a video of her freestyling went viral, news of her talent spread like wildfire. Everyone wanted a piece of this lyrical phenom. She's an extraordinary talent, and the youngest female rapper to ever sign a recording deal. If you guessed that my next guest is That Girl Lay Lay, then you guessed right. Let's go over and talk to her now."

The audience clapped, and the camera followed Charlene over to where she and I would sit and chat. She asked me the usual set of questions: How old are you? When did you first start rapping? Who are your favorite artists? How is it juggling school and fame? When she asked about school, that gave me the green light to tell her about the talent show and Hayes Theater.

Ms. Charlene was really interested in what I had to say.

"So, Lay Lay, tell me. Is there a place my viewers can go online to give to this cause? You know, I'm an alum of Rieger College and I used to act in the plays at Hayes Theater, so this is an important part of my history, too!"

"Oh, wow! That's so great." Then I tried to think fast about a place to give online. I got nothing. "Umm, I'm not sure if they can give online."

But Charlene Wilson came to my rescue.

"You know what, we have an old crowdfunding account," she told her viewers. "Team, can we get that on the screen? All proceeds go to save Hayes Theater. There, how's that?"

"That's great!" It was all I could say. I couldn't believe what was happening.

"Happy to help," Charlene said, smiling. "Now, will you perform a song for us?"

"Oh my gosh. Yes!"

I jumped up and walked over to the small stage. The music started, and I switched to beast mode. Performing in front of an audience is everything. Everybody got to their feet. I was a hit.

Charlene came over to me after I finished the song and gave me a big hug. "Lay Lay, you were amazing. Wasn't she just electrifying, everyone?"

The crowd roared.

"So much talent packed into this adorable little package. Lay Lay, will you promise me one thing? Okay, two: One, don't ever lose this confidence I see standing in front of me. Embrace your wonderful unique talent. And two, will you promise to come back on my show one day soon?"

"I sure will! Thank you, Ms. Charlene! Thank you, everybody!" I waved with both hands and gave a big smile.

The producer yelled, "Cut!"

With a few stops and starts, we made it through the segment in an hour. It was five thirty. My heart was sinking because of the time, but I also couldn't help but be so excited about being on-screen with Ms. Charlene!

As she and I walked off the set, Tasha came right up to us, beaming.

"Wow! You did so well, Lay Lay," Tasha said. "Ms. Wilson, we can't thank you enough."

"Please call me Charlene. Lay Lay tells me you just graduated from Samuelson School of Arts."

"Yes," Tasha said. I know she was feeling proud. "I majored in film."

"How wonderful! We need more bright women in film and television—in front of and behind the camera."

Then she turned to me.

"Lay Lay, you are just so wonderful. You have a big heart and big talent. You may find it hard to balance that sometimes, but your heart will always lead you to what's truest for you. Only you will know that truth. It may look different from what other people expect of you. Don't worry about that. You just stay true to what's in there." She pointed to my heart.

"Thank you, Ms. Charlene." She couldn't have known how right she was. "I had so much fun. This was like a whole dream come true."

"You got it, girl!" she said, and she gave me a high five. "My team will put together a clip from today's taping for social media. We'll get the word out right away about the theater. I promise we'll reach out as soon as we can with details on whatever funds we're able to raise. We'll try hard to save the Hayes."

"Thank you so much again, Charlene," Tasha said. "We'll look for that call!"

After saying our good-byes, we exited the building and made our mad dash to my school. It was already five forty-five. The school was more than forty-five minutes away. I was getting kind of nervous that Giana's worst fear would come to pass.

Ugh! We had to hurry.

·•✦·• CHAPTER 11 ·•✦·

"TASHA, CAN YOU GO ANY faster? I'm going to miss sound check."

"Oh, girl! You're gonna have to chalk that one up to the game. You have missed sound check at this point."

"No, don't say that."

"Lay Lay, I'm just trying to help you. You still have a chance to make it for the performance, though."

"Can you go any faster?"

"I wish I could, but this is how traffic is on a Friday afternoon," she said. "Trust me, I am going as fast as I can."

I sat back in the seat, feeling defeated. I couldn't see how we would make it in time. It was already nearing six o'clock—the time I was supposed to be there for sound check—and the GPS was saying we still had thirty-plus minutes to go. By now, I knew the girls were going to wonder where I was. I was starting to get nervous.

"Oh no! What's this?" Tasha said.

I saw red and blue lights ahead, and my stomach sank. It was an accident. We really couldn't handle any more delays, but this explained why we'd been bumper-to-bumper for the last few miles.

The GPS had adjusted our arrival time to 6:47, and I thought I was going to lose it. Then my cell phone rang. It was Riley.

"Hey, Lay Lay, where are you?" she asked. "We just got through with sound check. Are you on your way?"

"Yes! Tasha and I are stuck in traffic. There's an

accident. I'm not sure if I'll make it in time. What's the lineup? When do we go on?"

"They have us sort of in the middle, so even if you're a little late, you should be okay. You and Tasha just concentrate on getting here safely. Everything is going to work out. Don't worry."

Traffic had come to a complete stop now, and the GPS put our arrival time at seven fifteen. My heart was really beginning to pound now. *I'm going to miss the show.*

Tasha merged into the single lane traffic had been reduced to. As we passed the accident, we could see it was pretty bad. I hoped no one had been injured. I was also thankful we were finally on our way. Almost immediately traffic picked up to its normal peppy pace.

"Okay! Let's get it!" Tasha hollered, and we both laughed. I felt the tension in the car lift. She must have been glad to have the stress of getting through all that behind her, too.

"Oh my gosh! Lay Lay, you're here!" Riley was the first one to see me and Tasha running up behind the stone wall that shaped the back of the stage of our outdoor William Shakespeare Amphitheater. The wall gave us something like a backstage to hide behind.

"Hey, Lay! You made it. How did it go at *The Charlene Wilson Show?*" Akila asked as she came over on crutches to greet me.

It was seven fifteen. Oscar was onstage with his ferrets. I breathed a sigh of relief.

"It went really well. I can't wait to tell y'all about it."

I caught Giana's eye while I was talking, and she quickly looked away. *Ugh, she's still mad at me.*

"How are things here?" I asked quickly. "What's the plan?"

I looked right at Akila and her crutches. She glanced down at her ankle sadly.

"We went with the blinged-out chair option," Harper explained quickly, pulling a folding chair out from the side of the stage. She and the others had decked it out with sparkly ribbons and bows. I had to admit it looked pretty cute . . . for a folding chair.

"All right, Lay Lay," Tasha said. "Y'all are up next."

Oscar was just finishing up. It seemed that he did well. The crowd gave him some nice applause as he exited.

"Okay, everyone, give Oscar's ferrets another round of applause," Ms. Duncan said on the stage. "This next act is a group of five young ladies who you all know very well. Umm . . ." Ms. Duncan fumbled through her papers and looked offstage right at me. "Is one of you the lead?"

"Just say our names in alphabetical order," I whispered back.

"Right," Ms. Duncan said. "I know you'll enjoy this fivesome because they are singing and dancing to one of my favorite songs from the nineties— TLC's 'What About Your Friends'! Welcome to the Woodlawn Middle School stage, Akila, Giana, Harper, Lay Lay, and Riley!"

The audience clapped hard and quickly grew

quiet as we took our places. Harper carried Akila's diva seat to the middle of the stage and popped it open with Akila limping close behind her.

"Hey, everybody! I want y'all to stand up on your feet and get ready to rock with us," I shouted out.

Right on cue the music started, and whatever drama we had been through the last two weeks faded to the background. Everybody immediately knew what time it was.

We each sang and danced our parts so well, and everybody went wild. I know they had no idea. We killed the hook in our perfectly blended unison. It was so lit.

Harper sang us into the next verse. Then I came in. Suddenly, Akila jumped up out of her chair and started dancing—I was so surprised, I almost forgot my lyrics! Akila's moves were incredible. *When did we plan that?* I thought. I could tell the other girls were just as stunned as I was. *And wait, I thought she was hurt!* But, no, sis was ready.

The audience went wild!

The beat broke down, and we broke it down,

too, with the highlight of the choreo Akila had planned out perfectly.

Riley brought up the rear with a sweet lyric. We danced to the front of the stage and perfectly timed our diva poses at the end of the song. The place went wild. They wouldn't be talking about my friends as backup dancers anymore!

We were so happy, jumping and screaming and hugging one another. "Akila!" I shouted in the midst of the frenzy. "What in the world, girl? How did you pull off those moves? I thought you were still hurt."

"Well, I wanted to keep it a surprise from you all, but my doctor gave me clearance to perform for the show yesterday."

"You definitely had me fooled," Riley said.

"This was amazing, girls!" Ms. Duncan said. "Everybody, give them another hand." As if she had to ask. The crowd was going bananas.

Backstage, I found Giana. I knew I needed to apologize for being so bent on having it all and almost making a mess of such a big night.

When we locked eyes, we both said, "I'm sorry," at the same time. We laughed and I said, "You first."

"Lay Lay," she started. "I'm really sorry for being a hater. I mean, like, for real. What kind of friend have I been, making you pick between living your dreams and being happy with your friends? You shouldn't have to choose."

"Oh, no, Giana," I countered. "You were right. I was so set on having everything my way that I almost cost us this amazing night. What kind of friend was I? I may not have to choose between you and my new life, but I certainly do need to choose to be a better friend—one who listens when her girls are trying to check her."

"You have a point there," Giana said, only half joking. "But it wasn't all on you, Lay Lay. I was jealous, and I shouldn't have been. You have always been there for me, and I know there's room for me in the spotlight, too."

"Aw, girl, come here." I pulled Giana into a bear hug, and we laughed free and clear like old times.

Everything was going to be okay.

We broke out of the hug, and Giana smiled at me. "Let's go see what Reggie and them are talkin' about."

.·✦·. CHAPTER 12 .·✦·.

AFTER A FEW MORE SOLO acts and groups, Reggie and his crew ended the night. I'm not going to lie, they were fire. I was a little nervous for them. As a strictly rap group, could they keep the energy of their performance on point?

The answer to that came quickly as the boys moved around the stage like pros—well, semi-pros who were in middle school. They kept one another pumped while pumping up the crowd. They had put their money where their mouths were. That cypher energy hit different once they did it in front of an audience.

Soon, the night came to an end, and it was time to tally up the judges' votes. Who would win?

Reggie and Terrell came up to us while we waited for the result.

"So I see how it is," Terrell started in first.

"Oh yeah, what do you see?" Giana was ready for whatever kind of smoke they were thinking of bringing tonight.

"Naw, I mean, y'all are real good," Terrell said. "I ain't got nothing to say."

"Well, it's good to have you speechless for once, Terrell," Harper said.

"Something I haven't seen from you or Reggie since elementary school when you'd be put in time-out," I said.

"Whatever," Reggie said. "For real, though, I gotta give y'all your props. You really did good out there."

"Thank you," Riley said. "You guys were really good, too."

Ms. Duncan called all the acts onto the stage. She was ready to announce the winner.

"What an incredible night!" she said. "Don't we have some amazing talent here at our school?"

The audience clapped and cheered

"Okay, without further ado, let's find out who are our winners. Drumroll, please."

Everyone slapped their thighs really fast like they were congas. Then some kid from band jumped on the drums and hit the roll for real. The anticipation was building.

"The winner of the Woodlawn Middle School Talent Showdown is . . ."

I grabbed my friends' hands and squeezed them tightly.

"Akila, Giana, Harper, Lay Lay, and Riley!"

Ahhhh! We all screamed and jumped up and down. From the stage to the floor, everyone was clapping and cheering.

"Oh my gosh! We did it!" Giana said as we came together in a big group hug.

"While these ladies celebrate," Ms. Duncan said after a couple minutes of hoopla, "I want to let you know how grateful we are for having the most amazing parent and community support for the things we do with your kids here at Woodlawn. In addition to all that went into the talent show, we have an amazing cause we're supporting tonight. Part of the requirements for entering the Talent Showdown was for the kids to write a one-page essay nominating a local charity or cause that could use our help. Last week the entire school voted on the organization that would receive the funds from ticket sales, and Hayes Theater won."

The crowd clapped, and kids cheered.

"Hayes Theater has been part of our community for almost one hundred years and is facing possible closure and the demolition of its historic building. We can't let that happen. So we are honored to be able to play a part in preserving such an important part of Woodlawn history."

She paused so everyone could clap and show their support.

"From the ticket sales and even a few donations, we were able to raise fifteen thousand dollars for the Hayes Theater renovation project," Ms. Duncan continued. "However, I've learned from our winners that this is only a fraction of what is needed.

Demolition is set for tomorrow at eight a.m. unless the theater has fifty thousand dollars in hand to prove to the city that they can afford a complete renovation."

Soft boos swelled up from the crowd. This was really sad.

"We did an amazing job in the short time we had, but—"

Just then, we heard horns honking from somewhere near the front of the school. Three TV studio trucks were driving up on the grass toward the amphitheater. It was hard to see with their headlights shining at us, but it looked like one was a News Channel 19 truck and the other two were from *The Charlene Wilson Show*. I couldn't believe it.

Once they came to a stop, Ms. Charlene herself jumped out of one of the trucks with a megaphone. "Hey, I hear we have a theater to save."

I started screaming and jumping up and down. Everybody was in disbelief. What was going on?

"Earlier this afternoon Lay Lay taped a special segment on my show. She told me and all my viewers about our beloved Hayes Theater. We put together a clip for social media, and I challenged my fans to dig deep and give back to this theater that has meant so much to the city of Woodlawn. And do you know what? They came through."

The crowd roared.

"We collected twenty-five thousand dollars! But that's not all. I am going to match that twenty-five thousand dollars dollar for dollar."

"I'm going to faint," Tasha said to me.

We were all going wild. Ms. Charlene walked up to the stage with a giant check for $50,000. She literally saved the day.

My girls and I were a few of the last people to head home. Just before she left, Ms. Charlene came over to give her best to Tasha and me. We thanked her over and over again for coming in clutch like that. With her help, we literally took care of everything in one night! Even though I and the girls would still have a chance to perform our song on News

Channel 19 next week, we wouldn't have to worry about publicizing the plight of Hayes Theater at the same time. Ms. Charlene had been like a real-life fairy godmother, swooping in to save the day.

Tasha, Riley's mom, and Ms. Duncan were chatting it up not too far from us when I saw Akila walking toward us with five really pretty bags in matching pastel colors and patterns. I didn't even notice she had slipped away.

"Hey, Akila, whatcha got?"

"Well, I made a little something special for you and for our group."

"Ooh!" we all squealed.

She handed each of us a bag. We removed the tissue paper and each pulled out the drippiest hoodies I'd ever seen. They were jet black with a clear rhinestone-encrusted symbol of the number five and a star.

"Kee, what's this?"

"It's our name—FiveStar. The number five represents each of us and the ways we support our community in our own unique ways."

"This is amazing!" Riley said. "Maybe there are

more parts of our community that need saving."

"How in the world did you get this done so fast?" Giana asked.

"Don't worry about that. I have my ways." Akila laughed. "Do you like them?"

"Like them?" I asked, glancing at my girls. "We love them!"

"We can wear these when we do our winning performance on News Channel 19 next week," Harper said as she held up the hoodie in front of her.

This day had been the most beautiful almost-nightmare I'd ever had. The talent show win, Ms. Charlene's surprise appearance, plus my girls beside me the whole time had me feeling really good. Our friendship had been put through the fire these last few weeks, but we came out gleaming gold. I couldn't wait to see what my girls and I would be up to next.

Jevon Bolden writes, edits, and advocates for content for children and adults that opens them up to amazing ideas, diverse people, and rich experiences that stretch and inspire imagination. Jevon has a bachelor's degree in English from the University of Alabama and lives in sunny Florida with her family and cocker spaniel, Langston Hughes.